The Park Synagogue

ב״ה

RABBI RIDDLE

Written by Leibel Estrin
Illustrated by Dovid Sears

TABLE OF CONTENTS

The Jewish Holidays:

ISBN# 1-931681-74-0

Project Director: Rabbi Schneer Zalman Kalman Zirkind
Editor: Chaya Sarah Cantor
Proofreader: Natalie Zirkind
Graphics: Shazak Unlimited

Published by Shazak Unlimited
Brooklyn, NY
email: shazak@juno.com
Phone: (718) 771-8049

Distributed by Israel Book Shop
501 Prospect Street, Lakewood, NJ 08701
email: isrbkshp@aol.com
Phone: (732) 901-3009
Fax: (732) 901-4012

RABBI RIDDLE SAYS...
Sound the Ram's Horn!

Rosh Hashanah is the Jewish New Year. One of the things we do on Rosh Hashanah is blow the Shofar (ram's horn). The blast of the Shofar is a cry to G-d that is even higher than words!

"Hear" are some Shofar fun facts:

As a test, G-d asked Avraham to bring his son Yitzchak as a sacrifice. At the last moment, G-d commanded Avraham not to do so. Avraham then sacrificed a ram instead. We blow the Shofar every Rosh Hashanah to recall the merit of Avraham and Yitzchak, and thus to arouse G-d's merciful blessings for a good and sweet year.

What happened to you?

I tried blowing a ram's horn.

That doesn't explain how you got hurt.

Yes it does. The horn was still attached to the ram!

It is customary to blow trumpets whenever a new king is crowned. On Rosh Hashanah, we blow the Shofar to announce that G-d is our King.

Couldn't they have picked a flute instead?

We make three sounds on the Shofar: one long wailing sound called Tekiah, three short cries called Shevarim, and a chain of broken sobbing sounds called Teruah. They remind us to cry out over our mistakes and return to G-d!

What was the biggest mistake you ever made?

Thinking that I never made one!

We also recite lengthy prayers and extra psalms. This is because it is a day of judgment, when G-d reviews His creatures one by one, just as a shepherd reviews his sheep.

You and me, too!

That makes me feel a little sheepish!

On Rosh Hashanah, we do acts that symbolize our hopes for a good year. For example, we eat an apple dipped in honey so that our year should be sweet.

May you have a sweet year!

Even sweeter than honey!

Riddle What did one Shofar say to the other after Rosh Hashanah?

Answer on next page

5

Many people eat the head of a fish, to express their wish that in the coming year, the Jewish people may be a "head" and not a "tail."

What's wrong?

I can't tell which end is the head of the gefilte fish!!!

Toward the end of the first day of Rosh Hashanah (except when it falls on Shabbos), we visit a stream or pond and symbolically cast our misdeeds into the water.

YIPPEE !!!

You're supposed to throw your sins in the water. Not your snacks!

Answer from previous page
That was a blast!

REBBETZIN RIDDLE'S
STORY TIME

The Best Notes of All!

The Baal Shem Tov once called his follower, Reb Wolf Kitzis, to his study.

"Reb Wolf, I want you to blow the Shofar on Rosh Hashanah. To do so properly, please learn the mystical meditations that accompany this Mitzvah."

Reb Wolf studied the Kabbalah, then he took notes, so he could review them while he blew the Shofar. However, the Baal Shem Tov was not happy that Reb Wolf wrote down these secrets.

When Rosh Hashanah came, Reb Wolf frantically looked everywhere, but he could not find his notes! As a result, he felt that he would not be able to do the Mitzvah in the best possible way. With a broken heart and a humble spirit, Reb Wolf blew the Shofar without the mystical meditations, praying that G-d would accept his efforts.

When the prayer service was over, the Baal Shem Tov said to Reb Wolf, "Each gate to the King's palace has its own special key. But there is something that can open all the gates — an ax! So, too, each mystical secret opens one gate of Heaven. But you had a broken heart before G-d, and like a powerful ax, your tears broke through them all!"

RABBI RIDDLE SAYS...
Get Back to Where You Belong!

Yom Kippur means "Day of Atonement." We spend the entire day in prayer, asking G-d to forgive our mistakes and misdeeds. We do this by confessing and regretting the things we have done wrong, and resolving to do better in the future. Yet instead of feeling sad or depressed, we are happy — because just as we seek G-d's forgiveness, we know that G-d wishes to grant our requests. Therefore, Yom Kippur is actually the happiest day of the year!

!!!!

If G-d forgives us on Yom Kippur, so should you!

Riddle

Which fast is forbidden on Yom Kippur?

Answer on next page

Yom Kippur has five prayer services: Ma'ariv, Shacharis, Musaf, Minchah, and Ne'ilah. These correspond to the five levels of the Jewish soul — Nefesh, Ruach, Neshamah, Chayah and Yechidah. The holiest prayer service is the last one, Ne'ilah, which refers to the closing of the heavenly gates. It corresponds to the Yechidah level of the soul. This is a time when every Jew can discover his or her soul's essential connection to G-d!

How did the rabbi figure that out?

He did a lot of soul searching!

On Yom Kippur, we act like angels. Since angels don't eat, drink, wear leather shoes, wash or anoint themselves, neither do we!

Yom Kippur is such a gift from G-d. I'm happy that I'm a Jew!

I'm happy that I'm not an angel!

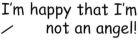

Answer from previous page

Break-fast!

REBBETZIN RIDDLE'S
STORY TIME

Sea for Yourself!

On Yom Kippur, we read the story of the Prophet Jonah.

G-d told Jonah to warn the people of Nineveh to correct their ways, or they would be punished. Jonah didn't want to deliver the message, because he was afraid that the people of Nineveh who did Teshuvah (mended their ways) would make the Jews who still had not done Teshuvah look bad. Then the Jews might receive a severe punishment.

Jonah tried to escape on a boat. However, G-d sent a giant storm to sink it. To save everyone, Jonah told the sailors to throw him overboard. When they did so, the storm ended! Meanwhile, Jonah began to drown. So G-d commanded a giant fish to swallow Jonah. It held him safely for three days, and then released him on the shore.

When Jonah delivered his prophecy to the king

of Nineveh, the ruler ordered everyone in his kingdom — even the animals — to fast and to change their ways. G-d then forgave the people of Nineveh. So may He forgive us!

RABBI RIDDLE SAYS...
United We Sit!

Sukkos is the Festival of Booths. It recalls the time when the Jewish people lived in fragile booths in the desert. Sukkos also recalls the Clouds of Glory that protected them. This holiday teaches us to have faith in G-d. Just as G-d protected and provided for the Jews in the desert, so He protects and provides for us today!

The Hebrew letters of the word "Sukkah" teach us how to build it! A Sukkah can have four sides like a Samech, three sides like a Khof, or two and a half sides like a Hey.

Hey Khof **Samech**

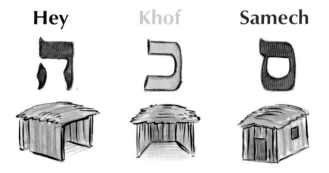

The most important part of the Sukkah is the S'chach, or covering. It must be made of plants or leaves that are no longer attached to the ground. Many people use bamboo or pine branches.

It is a Mitzvah to invite people into the Sukkah!

Mom, what's for dinner?

Stuffed cabbage!

How fitting!

The Sukkah symbolizes the time of Moshiach, when all people and all creatures will dwell together in peace.

Come in! There's room for everyone!

Riddle

When aren't you required to sit in a Sukkah?

Answer on next page

Besides dwelling in the Sukkah, we also make a blessing over four types of plants that grow near water: the Lulav (palm branch), Esrog (citron), Hadassim (myrtles), and Aravos (willows).

Just as we need all four species to perform the Mitzvah, so too, the Nation of Israel needs every type of Jew to be complete!

I'm important!

Me, too!

And so are you!

Answer from previous page
When you stand up for Kiddush!

16

REBBETZIN RIDDLE'S
STORY TIME

Chassidic Sukkah Decorations!

Many people beautify the Sukkah with dried fruits of the harvest, pictures of Jerusalem and the Holy Temple, verses from holy books, and other decorations. Others prefer the simple beauty of the Sukkah itself, so they do not decorate it at all.

Rabbi Chaim of Sanz had a special custom. Every year before Sukkos, he and his sons would collect money from community leaders and businessmen. They would give the money to poor people, to pay for their holiday needs. Rabbi Chaim and his sons also had lots of guests and learned Torah in the Sukkah.

One year, Rabbi Chaim was able to distribute a very large amount of money to the needy. As his young son entered the Sukkah, he saw that it seemed to glow with a special beauty. Yet not one decoration could be seen. "What makes this Sukkah so beautiful?" the boy asked.

Rabbi Chaim explained, "Many people decorate their Sukkos with all kinds of expensive ornaments. But my Sukkah is different. Its beauty comes from giving Tzedakah (charity) and performing acts of Chesed (kindness). This beauty is indeed special. Yet it is the kind of beauty that anyone can acquire!"

RABBI RIDDLE SAYS...
Happy Days are Here Again!

Shemini Atzeres is the "Eighth Day of Assembly," immediately following the seven days of Sukkos. It emphasizes the unique bond between G-d and the Jewish people.

Our Sages explain this with a parable. Once a king invited everyone to a banquet. After a week, most people went home. However, the king asked his close friends to stay an extra day, because it saddened him to see them leave. Similarly, G-d gave us this holiday right after Sukkos so that we would remain with Him a little longer.

On Shemini Atzeres, we begin to say a prayer for rain.

Why do we begin saying the prayer for rain now?

Because on this day, G-d "showers" blessings on the Jewish people!

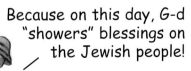

Riddle

What do teeth and the Torah have in common?

Answer on next page

On the night of Shemini Atzeres in Israel, and on the next night outside of Israel, we celebrate Simchas Torah. It is one of the happiest times in the entire year. We dance with the Torah to show our joy.

We also finish reading the Torah, then immediately start it all over again.

Are we at the beginning or the end?

Yes!

Answer from previous page

Wisdom!

REBBETZIN RIDDLE'S STORY TIME

The Power of Happiness!

Our Sages say, "Simchah Poretz Geder," or "happiness breaks through all boundaries." This true story shows just how important it is to be happy when we are serving G-d.

Once a Chassid had a son who was very ill. Although the Chassid had the best doctors and paid for the best medicines, his son did not get better. In fact, he seemed to get worse. By the time the holiday of Simchas Torah came, the doctors had given up hope. The man asked his Rebbe to bless his son so that he would have a complete recovery. The Rebbe told the father, "Soon it will be Simchas Torah. You must be joyful!"

The man was shocked. He had asked the Rebbe for a blessing, and instead he was told to celebrate Simchas Torah with joy! Although he surely didn't feel happy, he was determined to follow the Rebbe's advice. That Simchas Torah, he danced and danced. He forced himself to be happy, and to make others happy. When the holiday ended, the Rebbe called the Chassid over and said, "By serving G-d with joy, you have broken all boundaries — and you have saved the life of your son!"

So it was. The boy made a miraculous recovery. Today, he has children and grandchildren!

RABBI RIDDLE SAYS...
Flame On!

Chanukah celebrates the victory of the Jews over their Syrian-Greek conquerors during the days of the second Holy Temple, more than 2,000 years ago. The Greeks were not just military enemies. They wanted the Jews to forget that the Torah is holy. So they outlawed many of the Torah's signs of holiness, including Shabbos, Rosh Chodesh (first day of the new month), and Bris Milah (circumcision). Chanukah symbolizes this holiness, because it always includes Shabbos and Rosh Chodesh during its eight days. These eight days also correspond to the eight days before a Bris!

I hope the Greeks turn on their heels and run!

Why? Are you a professional soldier?

No, I'm a podiatrist!

The Jews were few, and the Greeks were many. But in the end, the Jewish soldiers defeated the Greek armies.

Please use "defeat" in a sentence.

When the Greeks lost the war, they used "defeat" to run away!

When the Jewish soldiers recaptured the Temple, they found enough pure oil to light the Menorah for only one day. Miraculously, the oil lasted eight days until new oil was brought. Today, we light the Chanukah Menorah for eight days to recall the miracles that G-d performed.

According to the Shulchan Aruch (Code of Jewish Law), a poor person should borrow or, if necessary, even beg money to buy candles or oil and wicks for Chanukah.

Can I have $156,000 for Chanukah candles?

$156,000 for Chanukah candles?

Yeah, I want to buy out the company that makes them!

The Menorah in the Holy Temple was filled with olive oil. Therefore, many people use olive oil for the Menorah's light. Oil floats on water. Similarly, no matter how much our enemies try to keep us down, the Jewish people always come out on top!

Why didn't you tell us that 2,200 years ago?

Riddle

What did one Dreidel say to another?

Answer on next page

The Dreidel children play with on Chanukah has its handle on top. The Grogger (noisemaker) that we use on Purim has its handle underneath. This teaches us that Chanukah expresses G-d's open miracles, while on Purim, the miracles are hidden — just as we are hidden in the costumes we wear!

Oops! I got it wrong!

Don't worry, your turn is coming!

On Chanukah, we add another candle each night when we light the Menorah. The Torah, too, is compared to light. Thus, Chanukah teaches us that we should always try to increase our learning of Torah.

We haven't finished yet!

Answer from previous page
Let's go for a spin!

REBBETZIN RIDDLE'S
STORY TIME

Show Me the Way Home!

One Chanukah, a Chassid decided to visit his Rebbe. It was a cold winter, but the thought of being with his Rebbe kept the Chassid warm.

Suddenly, snowflakes began to fall from the sky. Faster and faster, the flakes fell. The wind began to blow, swirling the snow in all directions.

The poor Chassid couldn't see the path. He couldn't see any landmarks. In fact, he couldn't tell if he was heading in the right direction or not.

Meanwhile, the sun had set. The Rebbe took a burning stick out of the stove, recited the blessings, and lit two candles. Usually, he sang or spoke words of Torah. But tonight, he just stared into the flames.

Back in the woods, the poor Chassid fell down in the snow. He was so tired, he wished he could go to sleep. However, he knew that falling asleep meant freezing to death. So he forced himself to get up and move on.

Suddenly, two lights appeared in the distance.
"Rescuers must be looking for me!" he thought.
The Chassid followed the lights through the
woods and fields. But he couldn't see a soul —
just the lights. He struggled on and on. Finally,
he saw the synagogue of his Rebbe.

The Chassid burst through the door and cried,
"Rebbe! Thank you for sending people to find me!"

For the first time that evening, the Rebbe
looked up. "I didn't send anyone," he explained.
"The light from the Chanukah candles must have
helped you find your way!"

And the truth is, the Chanukah lights still guide
us all!

AND WHILE WE'RE AT IT...
ANOTHER STORY!

A Woman's Liberation!

During the Jewish revolt against the Syrian-Greeks, there lived a woman named Yehudis, the daughter of Yochanan the High Priest. Yehudis's city was surrounded by the armies of General Holophernes. It didn't take long until there was very little food and water left.

"What are we going to do?" the people asked. "I have a plan," she replied.

That night, she went to the enemy camp. "Take me to your general," she told the guard. "I have an important message." She informed the general how he could conquer the city. He was thrilled. Later, she invited him to a dinner of wine and cheese. The general ate and drank so much that he fell asleep. Yehudis then took his sword — and cut off his head! Quickly, she gathered her things and hurried away.

When she got back to her city, she told Uziel, the captain of the Jewish forces, "Get ready to attack the Greeks. Their leader has fallen!" "What do you mean?" Uziel asked. Yehudis opened her basket. There was the head of General Holophernes. When the Greek army saw that their general had been killed, they quickly fled. Yehudis saved the town!

RABBI RIDDLE SAYS...
Don't Worry, Be Happy!

Purim recalls the miracle that occurred in the days of Mordechai and Esther when G-d saved the Jewish people from the wicked Haman.

Here are some more Purim fun facts:

Purim means "lots." Haman cast lots to pick the date to kill all the Jews. He picked Adar, the month when Moshe passed away. Haman thought it would be an unlucky month for us. But since Moshe was also born in Adar, it turned out to be an unlucky month for Haman!

What's a lot?

More than a little.

That's not a lot!

Then what is?

A lot is a ticket that's drawn in a lottery!

Why do we call the holiday "Purim?"

Because on this day, we have "lots" of fun!

G-d makes many kinds of miracles. Some miracles, like the splitting of the Red Sea, are very obvious. The miracle of Purim happened in a very hidden way. Yet our Sages say that it was one of the biggest miracles of all.

I had a miracle happen to me!

Oh yeah?

Yeah. I passed my science test!

On Purim, it's a custom to eat three-cornered cookies called Hamantashen. Some say the cookies are shaped like Haman's three-cornered hat. Others say that the three corners recall the merit of Avraham, Yitzchak and Yaakov.

What do you say?

I say that we eat Hamantashen because they're yummy!

We make noise when we hear the name of Haman read in the Megillah.

When I say Haman's name, make noise! Okay?

I'm ready!

Riddle What's the difference between Haman and the Jews who celebrate Purim?

Answer on next page

On Purim, it's a custom to wear costumes to recall the fact that Esther hid her Jewish identity from King Achashveirosh.

Mine is a "custom costume!"

In the Torah, Yom Kippur is also called "Yom Kippurim" — which can mean "a day like Purim." The holy Ari (Rabbi Yitzchak Luria) states that the closeness to G-d we can achieve on Yom Kippur by fasting, we can achieve on Purim by feasting!

I'll drink to that!

L'chaim!

Answer from previous page
Haman gets hung, the Jews get "hung-over!"

We have four special Mitzvos on Purim. They are:

1. Hear the story of Purim read from the Megillah, both at night and during the day!

2. Give charity to at least two poor people. Additionally, it is customary to give generously to all worthy causes.

3. Send a gift to at least one friend. It should contain two types of food you can eat right away, like a drink and some cake.

4. Have a special meal! It is a custom for adults to have wine or other drinks. But everyone should enjoy all sorts of good food.

On Purim, every kind of food tastes good!

We also say a special prayer thanking G-d for the miracle of Purim. This prayer is added to the Grace After Meals and the Amidah (standing prayer).

REBBETZIN RIDDLE'S STORY TIME

Do a Favor for Yourself!

Once Rabbi Sholom DovBer of Lubavitch asked his son Yosef Yitzchak to do a certain favor for one of the Chassidim. Later, Yosef Yitzchak returned and told his father, "I did the favor for the person, just as you asked."

"Thank you," his father replied. "But don't forget, G-d is the One Who truly helped the man. You simply agreed to become G-d's messenger."

The Rebbe then explained, "We find proof in the Megillah. Mordechai tells Esther, 'If you remain silent at this time (by not asking Achashveirosh to save the Jews), then relief and deliverance will come from elsewhere, but you and your father's house shall perish!'

"In other words," the Rebbe went on, "if you had not performed the Mitzvah, G-d would have found someone else — but you would have missed your opportunity."

RABBI RIDDLE SAYS...
It's Clean-Up Time!

Pesach, or Passover, celebrates our Exodus from Egypt and the "birth" of the Jewish people. On Pesach, it is forbidden to own any leavened products, known as "Chametz." So we clean our homes thoroughly to make sure there's no Chametz anywhere. That includes our rooms, our desks — even our pockets.

Wow! I never realized that cleaning your pockets could be so much fun!

POING!

We only have to clean places where we may have put Chametz.

Now you tell me!

To avoid owning Chametz on Pesach, we do three things: destroy (burn), verbally nullify, and sell it. (We store whatever we wish to sell in a special place, and then the Rabbi transfers ownership to a non-Jew for the holiday.)

Why do you want to own our chametz?

You mean boxtops?

Because I use it to collect something valuable!

No! I mean good deeds.

The Seder!

On the first two nights of Pesach, we take part in a special meal called the "Seder." During the Seder we read the Haggadah, which tells the story of the Exodus from Egypt. In this way, we fulfill the commandment, "And you shall tell your son on that day, saying, 'It is because of what G-d did for me when I went out from Egypt.'" It is a Mitzvah for each person to recite the Haggadah — but it is especially important to read it and discuss it with one's children!

The Haggadah has fifteen sections. This is similar to the fifteen steps leading up to the Holy Temple in Jerusalem. Each section takes us higher and higher!

What if you're afraid of heights?

Don't worry. On Pesach, we can only go up, not down!

Here is a short description of the fifteen sections:

Kadesh - We make Kiddush over wine to honor the holiday.

Urchatz - We wash our hands with a special cup.

Karpas - We dip green vegetables, onions, or potatoes in salt water. This represents the bitter tears of the Jews in slavery.

Yachatz - We break the middle matzah to remind us of how poor we were.

Maggid - We read the Haggadah that tells the story of Pesach.

Rochtza - We wash our hands before eating the matzah.

Motzi - First, we make the blessing that we usually say over bread.

Matzah - Then, we make a special blessing over the matzah and eat it.

Moror - We eat bitter herbs to remind us of the bitterness of Egypt.

Korech - We make a sandwich with matzah and bitter herbs to remind us of the way the great Sage Hillel used to eat the Pesach sacrifice.

Shulchan Orech - We eat a great meal!

Tzafun - We eat the last piece of matzah, called the Afikoman, to remind us of eating the Pesach sacrifice in the Holy Temple.

 **Berach -** We say the Grace After Meals.

 **Hallel -** We thank G-d for the miracles He performed in the past and will perform in the future.

 **Nirtzah -** We end the Seder with the wish that we meet in Jerusalem with Moshiach!

During the "Magid" section of the Haggadah, we read about the ten plagues that G-d inflicted on the Egyptians to punish them. Some people have a custom to spill out wine from their cups as they mention each one.

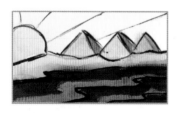 1. **Blood -** G-d turned the rivers of Egypt into blood.

 2. **Frogs -** Millions of frogs jumped all over the Egyptians.

3. **Lice** - These crawled all over the Egyptians.

4. **Wild animals** - All sorts of animals attacked the Egyptians.

5. **Dying animals** - A disease killed the Egyptians' domestic animals including horses, cows, donkeys, and camels.

6. **Boils** - Painful sores broke out all over the Egyptians' bodies.

7. **Hail** - Hail containing fire and ice smashed the crops.

8. **Locusts** - A huge cloud of locusts ate all the plants.

9. **Darkness** - It was so dark that the Egyptians couldn't move.

10. **Death of the Firstborn** - G-d killed the firstborn Egyptians, and also their firstborn slaves and animals.

The Haggadah begins with thanks and praises to G-d for taking us out of Egypt. It ends by expressing confidence that G-d will take us out of exile with Moshiach, speedily in our days!

We're ready!

Here are some of the things you'll need to celebrate the Pesach Seder:

Matzah

Hand-baked Shmurah Matzah. Shmurah means "guarded." The grain must be watched to make sure that it does not come in contact with water from the time it is harvested until just before baking.

We call this matzah "bread of poverty." Why?

Because we ate it when we were slaves.

Right! Any other reason?

A poor man feels humble. We are humbled by the miracles that G-d did for us — and continues to do for us!

Riddle
What did the baby grape say when it was squeezed before Pesach?

Answer on next page

47

Kosher wine or grape juice

We drink four cups during the course of the Seder.

What kind of cup do you have?

Right now, I have a hic-cup! Hic!

Maror / Bitter Herbs

We use Romaine lettuce, Belgian endives or horseradish. This reminds us of the bitter taste of exile.

How hot is it?

Say no more!

Answer from previous page
It didn't say anything. It just gave a little "wine!"

REBBETZIN RIDDLE'S
STORY TIME

Thoughts Count, Too!

The word "Haggadah" means telling. But *how* you read the Pesach Haggadah is just as important as *what* you say.

Once a great Rebbe, the Chozeh ("Seer") of Lublin, asked a wealthy man for a favor. "Please give my student, Reb Shmuel of Karev, everything he needs for Pesach."

The wealthy man did as the Rebbe asked. Reb Shmuel received new clothes for his entire family, pillows to lean on, the finest meat and fish, hand-baked Matzos in abundance, and vintage wine.

When the time came for the Seder, Reb Shmuel looked and felt like a king. Slowly, clearly, and with great enthusiasm, he read and discussed the Haggadah with the guests at his table.

However, Reb Shmuel was not used to the heavy food or aged wine. By the end of the next day's meal, he was very, very tired. Reb Shmuel took a nap, but he overslept.

When he finally awoke, he realized that he would have to rush. He ate and drank quickly and read the Haggadah without any extra discussion, just to finish on time. After it was over, he felt humbled and somewhat disappointed by the experience, especially when he compared it to the first night's Seder.

Some time later, he visited the Chozeh of Lublin. As he stepped into his study, the Rebbe said to him, "Reb Shmuel, you are mistaken! The second Seder was conducted out of simple desire to fulfill the Mitzvah. Therefore, it was received in Heaven more favorably than the first!"

RABBI RIDDLE SAYS...
"I-Witness" News!

Shavuos celebrates the giving of the Torah at Mount Sinai. At that time, over three million people, including 600,000 men over the age of twenty, witnessed this event! In addition, the entire world realized that G-d was giving the Children of Israel the Torah! Here are some fun facts about Shavuos:

When G-d gave the Ten Commandments, no creature made a sound, and there was no echo. This teaches us that everything on earth absorbed G-d's words. Therefore, our job is to uncover the holiness that already exists in the world. We do that by learning Torah and fulfilling the Mitzvos!

G-d wrote the Ten Commandments on two square tablets (called "Luchos") made of a blue jewel-like stone, and gave them to Moshe.

Our Sages compare Shavuos to a wedding. With the giving of the Torah, G-d "married" the Jewish people!

Shavuos is a happy day! Why are you so sad?

I'm not sad! I always cry at weddings!

Our Sages say: "Minhag Yisrael Torah He" — a Jewish custom is also part of the Torah. Here are some customs we follow on Shavuos:

To show G-d how much we love the Torah, we stay up all night in the synagogue and study. Many people read the "Tikkun Leil Shavuos." It contains sections from the Bible, Prophets, Holy Writings, Mishnah, and the Zohar.

The Zohar contains the Torah's mystical secrets!

No wonder I was mystified when I read it!

What are you learning?

I'm learning how to get along without sleep!

Riddle What's the best way to stay spiritually healthy?

Answer on next page

53

The Torah is compared to milk and honey, so on Shavuos, we eat dairy foods.

When Shavuos comes, what's the first thing you think of?

Cheesecake!

Shavuos is also known as Yom HaBikurim, the Day of the First Fruits. Farmers would bring their finest produce from the first harvest to the Holy Temple to thank G-d for all His blessings.

I hear that Abe's corn is terrific!

It 's so good, he's grinning from ear to ear!

Answer from previous page
Take two tablets every day!

54

REBBETZIN RIDDLE'S STORY TIME

The Torah Was Given for You!

Before G-d gave the Jewish people His Torah, He said to them, "Bring Me someone who can guarantee that you will keep it."

The Jewish people replied, "Let our Patriarchs, Avraham, Yitzchak, and Yaakov, be our guarantors!"

G-d replied, "As righteous as they are, they need guarantors for themselves!"

The Jewish people then said, "Let our Prophets be our guarantors!"

G-d replied, "They are indeed holy. But they, too, need guarantors of their own! Bring me others so that I can give you the Torah!"

The Jewish people said, "Let our children guarantee that we will always keep the Torah!"

G-d answered, "They are surely the best. I will

give you the Torah for their sake!"

So it was on the first Shavuos over 3,300 years ago.

So it is today. As our Sages say, "The entire world exists in the merit of the children who learn Torah!"

That includes *you!*